FARMER PARSNIP
FOOTBALL TRAINER

by Mary Newell
illustrated by David Pearson

Hippo Books
Scholastic Publications Ltd
London

Scholastic Publications Ltd, 141–143 Drury Lane,
London WC2B 5TG, England

Scholastic Book Services, 50 West 44th Street,
New York, NY 10036, USA

Scholastic Tab Publications Ltd, 123 Newkirk Road,
Richmond Hill, Ontario L4C 3G5 Canada

Ashton Scholastic, Box 579, Gosford,
New South Wales, Australia

Ashton Scholastic, 9–11 Fairfax Avenue,
Penrose, Auckland, New Zealand

First published by Scholastic Publications Ltd 1982
Copyright © Mary Newell 1982
Illustrations copyright © David Pearson 1982
All rights reserved

Colour separations by Acculith 76 Ltd, Barnet,
Hertfordshire. Printed and bound in Great Britain
by Balding + Mansell Ltd, Wisbech, Cambridgeshire

Farmer Parsnip was not always a football trainer. It all began one morning as he and Blossom were driving home from market where they had delivered the vegetables.

3

Rounding the corner, they saw a coach by the side of the road. A group of men were looking at a flat tyre.

4

Farmer Parsnip went to see if he could help. A man called Dave said that they were the Rangers football team on their way to play United in the cup final. How would they get to town in time? Farmer Parsnip offered to take them in the cart!

5

What an excellent idea! A happy team of players climbed into the cart and set off for town.

On the way they stopped at Toni's Garage. Farmer Parsnip explained what had happened, and Toni promised to have the tyre repaired and the coach outside the playing field by the time the match was over.

At last they arrived at the football ground. They were quickly shown to the changing rooms to get ready for the game.

Dave, the trainer, thanked Farmer Parsnip for his help, and invited him to stay and watch the match from the players' bench! Farmer Parsnip was delighted and readily accepted.

9

10 First he made sure Blossom was safe and happy. He left her on the rise overlooking the pitch, with a large bag of her favourite buns.

Then Farmer Parsnip took his seat alongside Dave and Terry,
the reserve player. He was proud and thrilled to be sitting there.
It was an exciting match.

11

12　There were near misses ... and spectacular saves.

Tackles ... headers ... and throw-ins ... but no goals!

Half-time came and went. Dave looked anxiously at his watch. It was almost full-time. Suddenly the players stopped playing. What had happened?

SCORE
UNITED 0
RANGERS 0

It was Blossom! Growing tired of being on her own, she had decided to join in the fun. She was good at heading the ball and almost scored a goal. The crowd laughed and cheered her.

15

A shame-faced Farmer Parsnip went to lead her off the pitch.

16   He made her stand still beside him while he watched the match.

Blossom must have inspired
the visiting team. With brilliant
passing, they broke through
the United defence.
The centre forward ran up
to shoot ...

17

... when crash! ... Much to the relief of the goal keeper he was sent crashing to the ground. The referee blew his whistle for a foul and awarded a penalty.

Dave grabbed the towel, and Farmer Parsnip the bucket and sponge, and they raced to the injured player.

And that was how Farmer Parsnip became a football trainer.
But only for a little while.
With Farmer Parsnip's gentle sponging, the player was soon
back on his feet and ready to take the penalty.

What a penalty it was! Straight into the back of the net. As fast
as a cannon ball. Nobody could have stopped it. The referee blew
the whistle for goal and full-time. The crowd cheered.

There was more cheering as Rangers received the County Cup from the Mayoress.

Then the Rangers cheered Farmer Parsnip and Blossom.
They made Farmer Parsnip honorary trainer for all
the help he had given. He was proud.

Once again, Farmer Parsnip and Blossom set off home.
Farmer Parsnip thought of the tale he had to tell the
animals this time. They would never believe he had
been a football trainer. Or would they?